The Rainbow Fairies

To Wilson, who fills each day with color

Special thanks to Kristin Earhart

Library of Congress Cataloging-in-Publication Data is available.

ISBN 978-0-545-22291-4

10 9 8 7 6 5 4 3 2 1   10 11 12 13/0

Printed in the U.S.A. 40
First printing, January 2010

The Rainbow Fairies

By Daisy Meadows

Cartwheel BOOKS®

SCHOLASTIC INC.

New York   Toronto   London   Auckland
Sydney   Mexico City   New Delhi   Hong Kong

It is a special day in Fairyland.
Today is the Feast of All Colors,
so the Fairy King and Queen
are having a picnic to celebrate.

YOU ARE
INVITED TO
The Feast
of All
Colors

All the fairies are excited, especially
the Rainbow Fairies.

Inky
the Indigo
Fairy

Amber
the Orange
Fairy

Fern
the Green
Fairy

Sunny
the Yellow
Fairy

They get to choose the foods for the picnic.
There are seven Rainbow Fairies, one
for each color of the rainbow.

Ruby
the Red
Fairy

Heather
the Violet
Fairy

Sky
the Blue
Fairy

They are sisters, and they share an
important job:
to fill the world with color!

The Rainbow Fairies are busy in
their toadstool cottage.
It is almost time to fill the picnic baskets.

Just then, the fairy sisters
hear a knock at the door.

"Hello, Rainbow Fairies," a voice croaks.

"Bertram!" the sisters exclaim.

Bertram the frog is a royal messenger and
also their good friend.

"The king asked me to clean your
wands," says Bertram.
"Of course," Ruby replies.
"They need to work well for the feast,"
Inky agrees.

The fairies hand their wands to Bertram,
who wipes them with a magic cloth.
As the fairies talk about the foods they will
pick, Bertram's stomach growls.

"Excuse me," says the frog.
"I can't wait for the picnic!
The food will be delicious!"

Bertram returns the wands to
the fairies, one by one.

But he isn't thinking about wands,
he is thinking about the feast.

"Thank you, Bertram," the fairies say.

"I am happy to help!" he replies.

"I'll see you at the picnic!"

The fairies carry the empty picnic baskets
outside to the meadow.
"What a beautiful day for a picnic!" Fern
exclaims.

"But it isn't a picnic without food,"
insists Sunny.
Heather says, "Let's get started!"

"I'll go first," says Ruby.
She thinks of her favorite red foods.

"Strawberries, tomatoes, and cherries!" Ruby
says.
Sparkles stream from her wand into one of
the picnic baskets.

Now it's Amber's turn.

She flicks her wand.

"Sweet potatoes, carrots, and tangerines!" she calls out.

"I'm next," says Sunny.
"Corn on the cob with butter! And
lemonade!"
Sparkles stream into the basket.
"Now for green," Fern says. "Broccoli, peas,
and cool cucumber soup, please!"

"Blueberry pie!" Sky declares happily.

"Blackberries!" sings Inky.

"Grape jelly!" exclaims Heather.

Sparkles fly from their wands and spin through the air.

"Hooray!" cry the fairies. "The picnic is ready!"

"Let's go home and wash up before the feast," Ruby says.

Just as the fairies leave, someone arrives early for the feast.

It's Bertram, and he's hungry!
He tiptoes up to a picnic basket, lifts the
cover, and looks inside.
"Oh, no!" he cries.

Ruby rushes out of the cottage. "What's the matter, Bertram?"
Bertram points to the baskets and Ruby looks inside.
"Red corn on the cob? Blue strawberries? Violet tangerines?" she mumbles.

"What went wrong?" Bertram asks. "That food does not look delicious."

Ruby's eyes grow wide. "We must have used the wrong wands!" she realizes. "I have to call my sisters!"

Ruby points her wand straight up and blue sparkles shoot into the air.

Soon, the other Rainbow Fairies return to the meadow.

"We got back the wrong wands after Bertram cleaned them," Ruby explains. "And the picnic foods are all the wrong colors!"
"Can we fix it?" Sky asks.

"We need to work together," Ruby says. "We need Rainbow Magic! And fast! The king and queen are coming!"

At once, the sisters make a circle.

They hold their wands up high and speak
together:
"Rainbow colors, bold and bright,
The picnic foods are just not right.
Now each wand must find its fairy
And fix the shade of each grape and berry."

The wands spin around in the air, and
each one lands in the hand of its fairy.
Just then, sparkles of every color shimmer
and swirl through the meadow.

"What a beautiful beginning to the Feast of All Colors!" announces the king.
"The food looks delicious," the queen says.

"Yes, it does," agrees Bertram, winking at the Rainbow Fairies.
Everyone sits down to enjoy a colorful feast.
They have a lot to celebrate!